D0382690

The Day That Henry Cleaned His Room

Sarah Wilson

SIMON & SCHUSTER BOOKS FOR YOUNG READERS
Published by Simon & Schuster
New York London Toronto Sydney Tokyo Singapore

SIMON & SCHUSTER BOOKS FOR YOUNG READERS
Simon & Schuster Building, Rockefeller Center
1230 Avenue of the Americas, New York, New York 10020

Copyright © 1990 by Sarah Wilson. All rights reserved including the right of reproduction in whole or in part in any form. SIMON & SCHUSTER BOOKS FOR YOUNG READERS is a trademark of Simon & Schuster. Manufactured in the United States of America

10 9 8 7 6 5 4

(pbk) 10 9 8 7 6 5 4 3

Library of Congress Cataloging-in-Publication Data
Wilson, Sarah. The day that Henry cleaned his room. Summary: When Henry cleans his room, he attracts the attention of reporters, scientists, the army, and something long and green and scaly that lives under Henry's bed. [1. Cleanliness—Fiction. 2. Orderliness—Fiction.] I. Title.
PZ7.W6986Day 1990 [E] 89-11571

ISBN 0-671-69202-X ISBN 0-671-87168-4 (pbk)

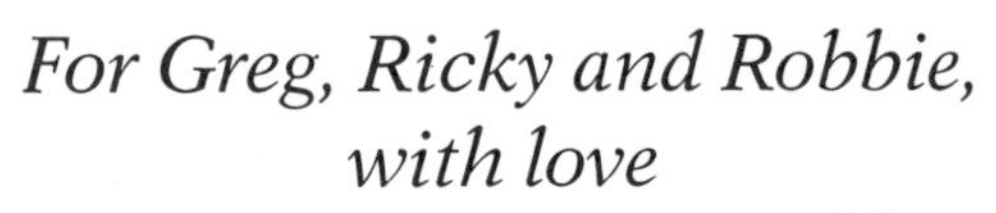

For Greg, Ricky and Robbie,
with love

KQIP
9

The day that Henry cleaned his room, reporters came.

Henry got up early.

"I know I can do it this time," he said.

Henry's mother and father cheered.

So did his little sister Lou.

It had been a year since anyone had seen the inside of Henry's room. Henry was the only one who knew the secret path from the door to his bed.

"Okay," Henry yelled from his bedroom door, "everybody out!"

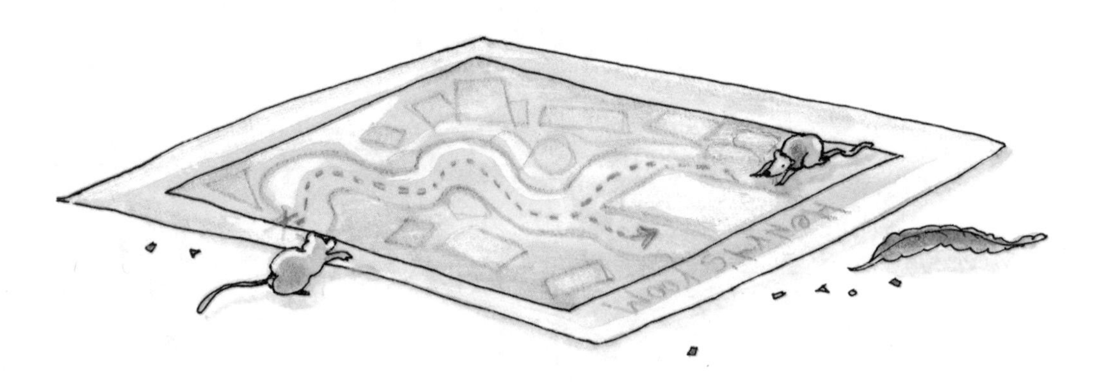

STOP
POPCORN
CRISPY OATS
SODA
JUICE
SODA
TOMATOES
AGE 2
POEM
SOAP
NOODLES
ERASERS

The first ones out were Henry's fish. It had been so long since Henry cleaned their tank that they had grown long legs and climbed out, preferring air to dirty water. They scowled at Henry and walked down the stairs.

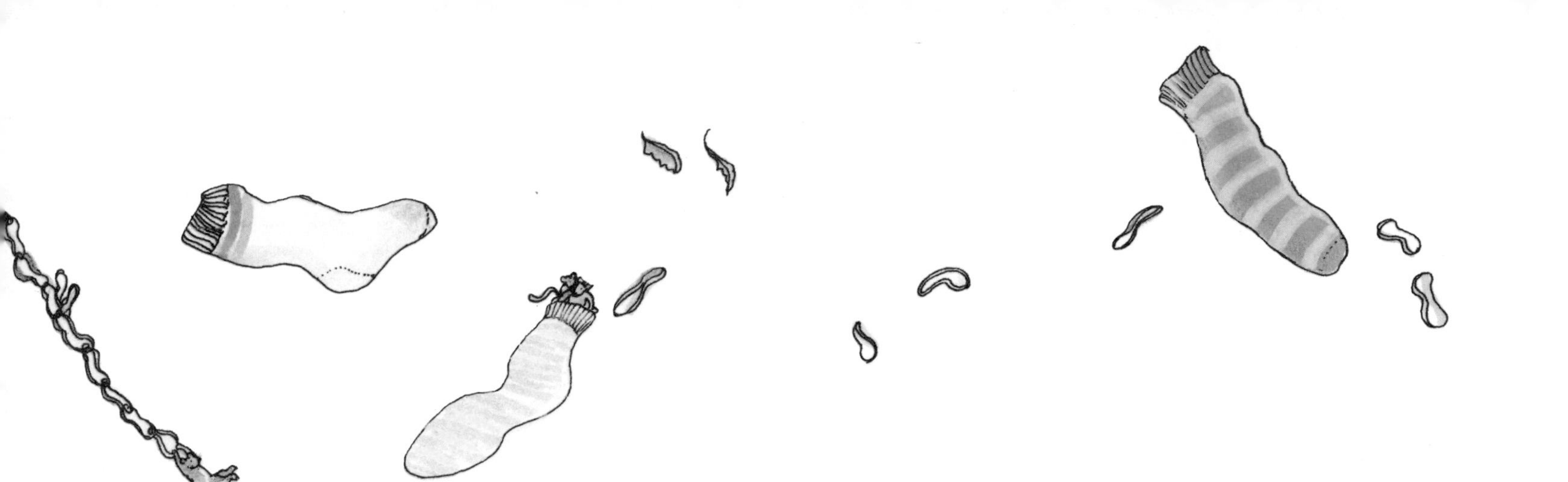

The mice came next. They brought out Henry's collections of mismatched socks and rubber bands. They weren't happy about moving.

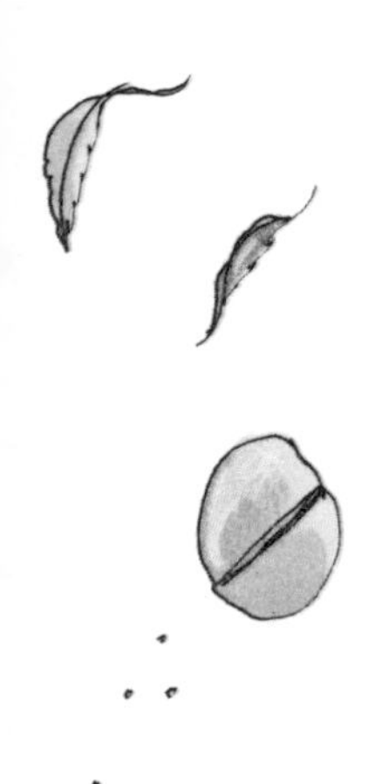

The raccoons came after them. They carried Henry's collections of corncobs, stale hamburger buns, cereal boxes, and feathers.

Henry's mother was shocked. "Who *are* those animals," she asked. "And why are they all so *big*?"

"Henry's friends," said his father. "He's kept them well fed."

A flea circus came out of Henry's room and did cartwheels down the stairs.

"I knew there'd be bugs in there," said Henry's sister Lou.

A possum rode
out wearing Henry's
Hawaiian shirt.
"I'd wondered
where that went,"
said Henry's mother.

Finally, something long and green and scaly slithered out from under Henry's bed and ran down the stairs.

"What was THAT?" Lou gasped.

Henry was puzzled. "I don't know," he said. "Must be somebody's friend who stayed over."

STOP
JUICE
SODA
ICE CRE

JUST-SO
STORIES

With everyone out of his room, Henry started the real work.

The army took away his parachutes.

1928
TOMATOES

The Historical Society took his collection of old bottles and cans.

Henry's scout troop took the old newspapers and magazines.

"Wow!" said Henry. "I can see the window now!"

It was hard going, but Henry kept at it.

SPECIES
ICE CREAM
SPECIMENS

Scientists came to study the different kinds of dust and must and moss and mushrooms that were growing out of Henry's closet and walls.

Suddenly, Henry found a new window.

Birds he'd never seen flew out of his closet and took off for the open sky.

CAMPCRAFT
PAINTS
KITTY

He found the bathrobe his Aunt Skooky had given him for his third birthday. He found his bicycle. He found birds' nests and beach pebbles and old crayons and tennis shoelaces.

Henry washed and wiped and scrubbed and polished.

CAMP
PUZZLE
Rocks

Outside, his family had a big yard sale of all the things Henry didn't want.

His mother helped him change his bed sheets, and then...

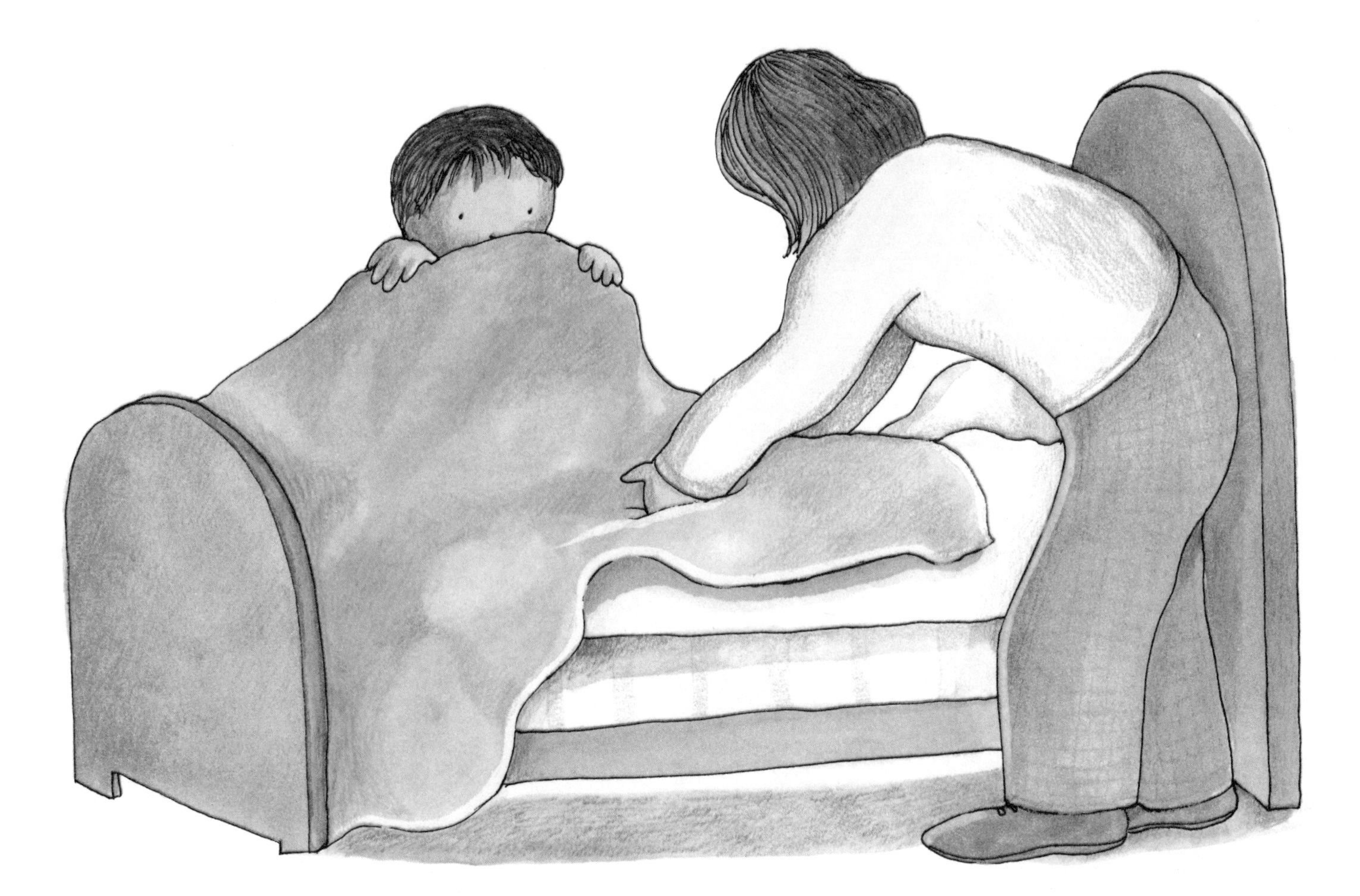

Henry spoke on television. "I did it!" he shouted. "I have a *clean* room!"

Everybody cheered.

Henry was the talk of the neighborhood.

CLEAN
KQUP

When night finally came and everyone had gone home, Henry went up to his clean room. He got into his clean bed, but he couldn't sleep. He could see walls and windows and even the door to his room. "It's so EMPTY!" Henry wailed.

"You'll get used to it, dear," said his mother and father.

"I *like* a clean room," said his sister Lou.

But Henry lay awake staring into the dark until he heard the squeak of a window slowly opening.

CRISPY
OATS

One by one, his old friends tiptoed back into the room, except for one long, green, scaly something that slithered under Henry's bed.

They all carried something. Socks. Rubber bands. Corncobs. Cereal boxes. Feathers.

They spread out comfortably on the floor.

"At least *I'm* not doing it," Henry said.

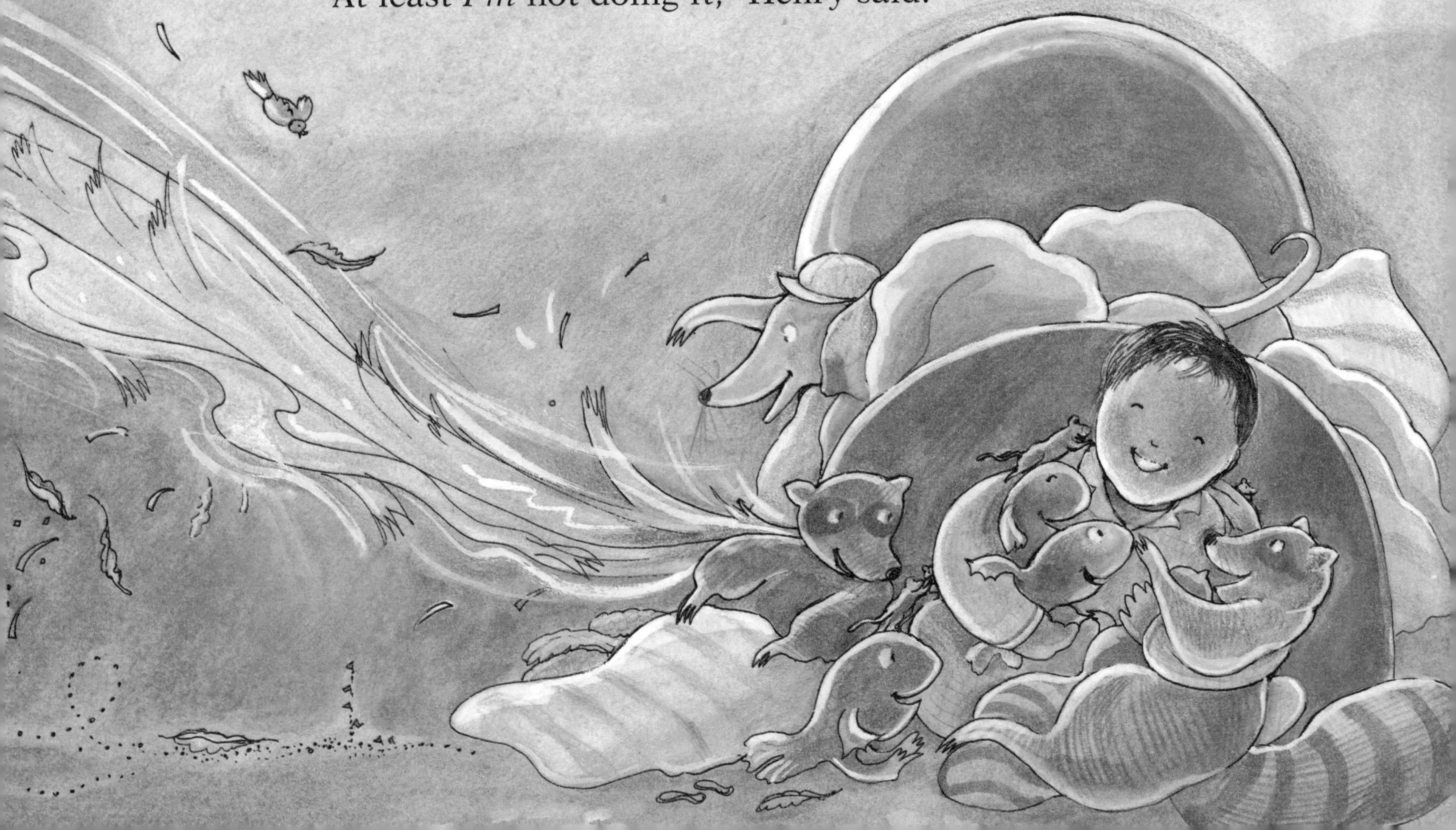

When Henry's room was nice and messy again, everybody curled up in a cozy place to sleep.

They were all very happy.

It must be the clean room, Henry thought.

And then he fell asleep, too.

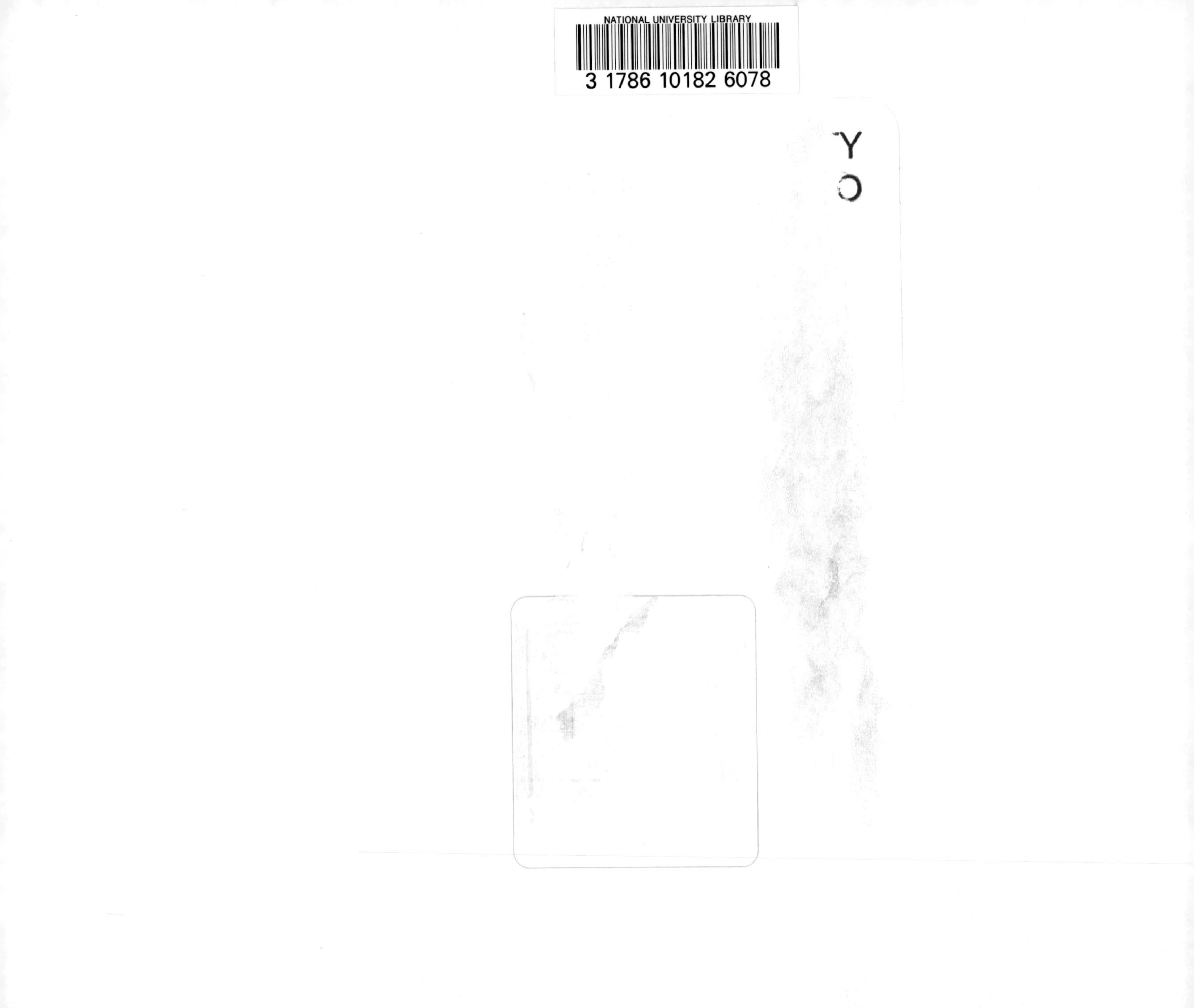

NATIONAL UNIVERSITY LIBRARY
3 1786 10182 6078